Disney

MICKEY MOUSE CLUBHOUSE

CHOO CHOO EXPRESS

By Sharon Fass Yates
Illustrated by Loter, Inc.
Based on the episode by Mark Seidenberg

Disney PRESS

New York

Hi, everybody! Welcome to the Clubhouse!

It sure is hot today! We're trying to think of ways to stay cool.

Minnie's dreaming about snow. Brrr . . . I feel cooler already!

Can you think of something fun to do with snow? Lift the flap to find out!

"I have a supercool idea!" Mickey says. "Do you remember Professor Von Drake's Icy Cold Easy-Freezy Snow?"

"You mean the snow that stays cold and never, ever melts?" asks Minnie.

"Yup," answers Mickey.

But where is the Professor's snow?

"If only we could bring the snow to the Clubhouse," says Mickey.

"But Mistletoe Mountain is far away," Minnie says. "How can we get there? And how can we take heaps of snow back to the Clubhouse?"

"Let's look in the garage," says Mickey. "We might find something to help!"

Do you see something that could work?

"Let's get choo-choo-chooing," says Donald. "*Allll aboard!*"

"But Choo Choo needs tracks to ride on," Mickey says. "They're in a box in the shed."

"I found a box!" calls Donald. "Aw, phooey," he says as the box slips.

Mickey says, "We need these springs to spring back into their box. Oh, Toodles!"

"Let's see what tools Toodles has for us," says Mickey.
Which Mouseketool do you think will work?

"Now Choo Choo is ready to go," says Mickey. "All aboard!"

As they roll along, Minnie sings, *There's nothing better than choo-chooing!*"

"We're almost at the mountaintop, but why did Choo Choo stop?" Daisy asks.

"There's a river in the way. How can we cross it?" asks Goofy.

"Maybe Toodles can help," replies Mickey. "Oh, Toodles!"

We used the magnet, but how can a ladder help?

"Hiya, Professor," says Mickey when they reach the top of Mistletoe Mountain. "It's such a hot day, we thought we could bring your Easy-Freezy Snow to the Clubhouse."

"But how can we scoop up all this snow?" asks Goofy.

Mickey says, "Everybody call, 'Oh, Toodles!'"

It's time to pick the Mystery Mouseketool—but what could it be?

After the snow is in Choo Choo's cars, the gang heads back to the Clubhouse.

"My snow never melts, so you can play in it anytime!" the Professor exclaims.

"A-hyuck! I'm an angel!" says Goofy.

"I wonder where Minnie and Daisy could be?" says Mickey.

Let's look and see!

Thanks, everybody, for helping to bring Professor Von Drake's Icy
Cold Easy-Freezy Snow to the Clubhouse.
See you real soon! And until then—stay cool!

MISTLETOE MOUNTAIN MAZE

Help Mickey and the Choo Choo make their way to Mistletoe Mountain so they can pick up the Easy-Freezy Snow.

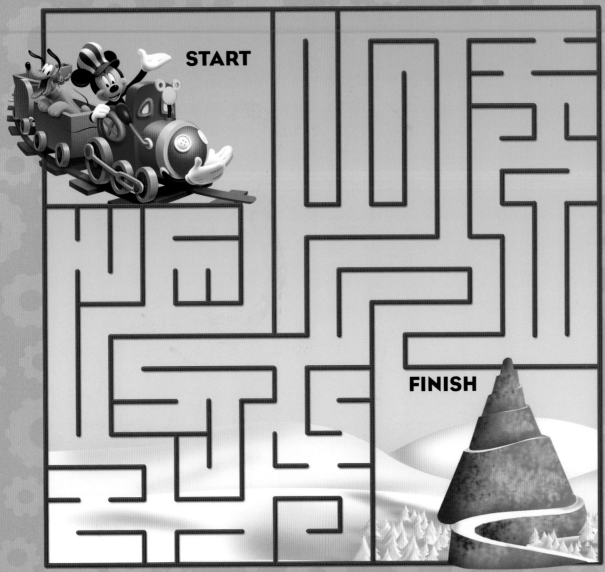

START

FINISH

STICKER FUN!

Use your stickers and have fun filling up this snowy scene!

SPOT THE DIFFERENCES

Can you spot 10 differences between the picture on the left and the picture on the right?

SHADOW MATCH-UP

Draw a line from each character to its matching shadow.

Read the story again and try to find these 10 items. Check off the box next to each item when you find it!

- ☐ Professor with hands on hips
- ☐ Snowman's top hat
- ☐ Pluto in engineer's hat
- ☐ Basketball
- ☐ Elephant shooting snow
- ☐ Magnet with springs
- ☐ Toy tricycle
- ☐ Minnie's orange fan
- ☐ Toy car
- ☐ Snowman's carrot nose

Check out these other books featuring Mickey Mouse and the Clubhouse Gang!